KV-191-311

IMAGINE THAT™

Licensed exclusively to Imagine That Publishing Ltd
Tide Mill Way, Woodbridge, Suffolk, IP12 1AP, UK
www.imaginethat.com
Copyright © 2022 Imagine That Group Ltd
All rights reserved
4 6 8 9 7 5 3
Manufactured in China

Written by Susie Linn
Illustrated by Gal Weizman

All rights reserved. No part of this publication may be reproduced, stored in a retrieval system, or
transmitted in any form or by any means, electronic, mechanical, photocopying, recording or otherwise,
without the prior written permission of the publisher. Neither this book nor any part or any of the
illustrations, photographs or reproductions contained in it shall be sold or disposed of otherwise than as
a complete book, and any unauthorised sale of such part illustration, photograph or reproduction shall be
deemed to be a breach of the publisher's copyright.

ISBN 978-1-80105-300-6

A catalogue record for this book is available from the British Library

Kisses and Wishes

Written by Susie Linn

Illustrated by Gal Weizman

Every bedtime, mummy dragon tucked little Finn up nice and cosy. 'A kiss and a wish, then off to sleep!' she said.

Mostly, Finn wished for simple things, like having his best friend Roary to play. Or his favourite cheese toastie for tomorrow's breakfast.

But one bedtime, Finn decided
to wish for something a little bit
different. 'I'm a dragon,' he said to himself,
'and dragons should be brave and try new things!'

'A kiss and a wish, then off to sleep!'
said Mummy. Finn was ready with his wish.

'I wish I could stay up **ALL** night!' he said.
And to his surprise, Mummy said 'yes'!

That night, Finn got
up to lots of fun ...

... and lots of
mischief!

But the next morning he had to go to school and he felt terrible!
Staying up all night was great, but it made Finn very tired, too.

'A kiss and a wish,
then off to sleep!'
said Mummy
the next night.

Finn was ready with his second brave wish. 'I wish I didn't
have to go to school tomorrow!' he cried, excitedly.
And again, to his surprise, Mummy agreed!

But Finn was lonely without his friends to laugh and play with all day.

'A kiss and a wish, then off to sleep!' said Mummy the next night.

Finn was ready with his third brave wish. 'I wish I could watch my favourite shows **ALL** day!' And would you believe it, Mummy said 'yes'!

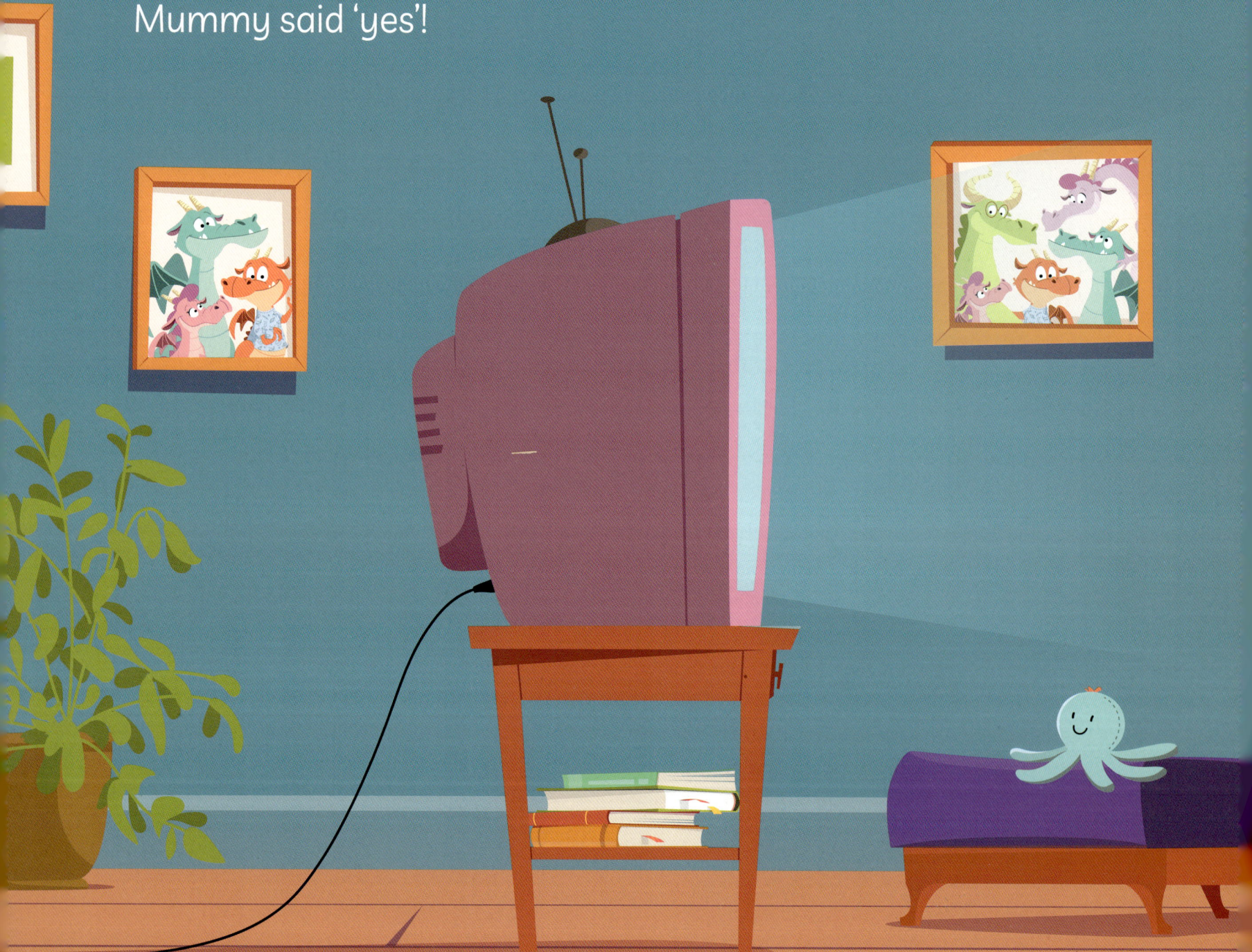

But there were no TV snacks for Finn to eat and he became **very** hungry indeed.

The next night, at kiss-and-wish time, Finn wished that he could eat exactly **what** he wanted …

… **as much** as he wanted …

... **whenever** he wanted!

Uh-oh! That was a big mistake. Finn ate **way** too much.

Although Mummy kept saying 'yes' to all Finn's bedtime wishes, things were not turning out quite the way he imagined.

The next night, Finn wished that he never had to take a shower ... ever again. But that didn't go very well either! It was time to try something else.

Finn wanted a new name. 'Imagine calling a dragon *Finn!*'
he said to himself. 'What about a cool dragon name,
like *Blaze, Flame, Sparky* or *Tiger?*' He had a little think.
'Well, maybe not *Tiger!*'

Blaze
Flame
Sparky
Tiger

Great Dragon Names

'A kiss and a wish, then off to sleep!' said Mummy that night. And Finn was ready with his new-name wish.

The next day was Finn's birthday and the postman arrived early with a big bag of cards and presents. They were all addressed to *Finn*.

'No ... there's nobody called *Finn* here!' said Daddy to the postman. 'We have a *Blaze*, but not a *Finn*.'

'Oh dear,' said the postman. 'Then I must take these cards and presents away.'

Finn began to cry. 'Mummy,' he sniffled, 'may I have my kiss and wish now, instead of at bedtime?' Mummy nodded.

'I wish to be *Finn* again,' said Finn, 'and for everything to be just the way it used to be.' And of course, Mummy said 'yes'.

Just in time, Daddy called the postman back.
'You can leave the cards and presents after all!' he said.

That night, Finn got an extra
birthday kiss and wish at bedtime.

'A kiss and a wish, then off to sleep!'
said Mummy, giving Finn a big hug.

'I'd **LOVE** my favourite cheese toastie for
breakfast tomorrow,' wished Finn.

'Yum, yum, **YUM!**' said Finn at breakfast time. He had learned that he had so much to be grateful for.

Sometimes, simple wishes
are the very best!